PIPPA'S PON

Tea

Hi Everyone

I've been busy with all my horses this year but I'm delighted to share these stories about Tilly and her beloved horse, Magic Spirit. Still part of my *Pippa's Pony Tales* series, they focus on Tilly and Magic's partnership as they work together and compete at a higher level. Tilly's way of riding reflects my way of riding. The advice that Tilly is given is what I would teach, and it's how I've been taught. Over my career it's what I have found has worked for me as I've competed with my horses, so I hope you find it useful. Most of all I hope you enjoy reading Tilly and Magic's adventures as much as I have enjoyed writing them.

Keep reading, keep riding and follow your dreams!

See you soon,

Also by Pippa Funnell

Magic Spirit the Dream Horse
Red Admiral the Racehorse
Rosie the Perfect Pony
Samson the Stallion
Lucky Chance the New Foal
Solo the Super Star
Pride and Joy the Event Horse
Neptune the Heroic Horse
Parkview Pickle the Show Pony
Nimrod the Circus Pony
Moonshadow the Derby Winner
Autumn Glory the New Horse
Goliath the Rescue Horse
Buttons the Naughty Pony
Rusty the Trustworthy Pony
Royal Flame the Police Horse
Stripy the Zebra Foal
Free Spirit the Mustang
Team Spirit
Team Training
Team Work

PIPPA'S PONY TALES

Team Magic

Pippa Funnell

ZEPHYR
An imprint of Head of Zeus

This is a Zephyr book, first published in the UK in 2025
by Head of Zeus Ltd, part of Bloomsbury Publishing Plc

9 7 5 3 1 2 4 6 8

A catalogue record for this book is available from the British Library.

ISBN (PB): 9781837933518
ISBN (E): 9781837933495

Typeset by Nicky Borowiec

Printed and bound in Great Britain by
CPI Group (UK) Ltd, Croydon CR0 4YY

FSC
www.fsc.org
MIX
Paper | Supporting responsible forestry
FSC® C013604

Bloomsbury Publishing Plc
50 Bedford Square, London, WC1B 3DP, UK
Bloomsbury Publishing Ireland Limited,
29 Earlsfort Terrace, Dublin 2, D02 AY28, Ireland

HEAD OF ZEUS LTD
5–8 Hardwick Street
London EC1R 4RG

To find out more about our authors and books
visit www.headofzeus.com
For product safety related questions contact productsafety@bloomsbury.com

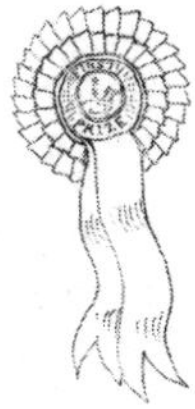

For the most important person
in my life, William, who is not only
my husband, but my best friend and
who shares the same undying
passion for horses that I have.

One

'She makes it look easy,' said Tilly, sounding agitated. 'How *does* she do it?'

Her eyes were glued to the small television that sat on top of the trophy cabinet in Silver Shoe Farm's clubhouse. She was watching her eventing heroine, Livvy James, riding her chestnut gelding, sail over a trakehner at last year's Bramham Horse Trials.

The jump was a real rider-frightener – a huge log suspended over a deep, wide ditch. The fence was intimidating enough, with the enormous ditch, but it was made worse by the fact it was positioned at the entry to a wood with a big drop on the landing side. Tilly could understand why riders might be tempted to override these fences, because they look so intimidating, but for a horse they were really straightforward jumps.

Tillly felt she was making too much of an issue of it in her head. Her imagination made the ditches wider and deeper, but she knew this was a mindset she had to overcome.

She rewound the footage and played it again. Just as she leaned closer to the screen, determined to spot her heroine's secrets to success, Angela, Silver Shoe Farm's owner, came in with two mugs of hot chocolate.

'Trakehners, again?'

Tilly frowned.

'I need to study the speed Livvy approaches at. There's bound to be a trakehner at the event this weekend and I don't want to have a problem if I'm to have any chance of being selected for the Regional Team.'

'Oh, yes, the Under 18 Championships at Weston Park,' said Angela. 'They're coming up soon, aren't they? I completely forgot that it includes the Regional Team Championships.'

'At the end of the month,' said Tilly. 'They'll be picking the team based on this weekend's competition. I know Magic and I are more than capable of getting selected if all goes well.'

'If it's the trakehner you're worried about, we'll go out and practise as soon as you're ready.'

Duncan had made one recently. A tree had come down in a storm earlier in the year and with help from Angela's father he'd placed it over the ditch that ran along the bottom of the long field.

'Thanks,' said Tilly.

She sipped her hot chocolate and tried to think positively. She appreciated Angela's offer. Angela had plenty of competition experience and always gave the best advice. Nonetheless, Tilly's unease about the Weston Park selection was bothering her. In her heart, she knew she could overcome her anxiety with trakehners. What she couldn't conquer, however, was the terrifying prospect that any day now, her horse, Magic Spirit, might be taken away from her.

It had been a while since Tilly had received the first threatening email from Fred Webb, a farmer, who claimed Magic belonged to him and that he had the paperwork to prove it. Tilly had tried to ignore his messages at first, hoping Fred Webb would just go away.

But he didn't.

He wanted Magic back – despite the fact that he'd abandoned the poor grey at a roadside some years before. Tilly feared he was only interested because he'd realised Magic was worth something now, having been featured in local papers and riding magazines as a potentially top-class event horse, a novice to watch out for. Fred didn't care about Magic's welfare. He just wanted to make money.

It was Tilly who'd nursed Magic back to health, Tilly and the team at Silver Shoe Farm who'd had the patience and passion to train him. And it was Tilly who'd formed the intense bond with him. The thought of that being broken was like someone slowly breaking her heart in two. The worry stayed with her constantly: morning, noon and night. Even so, she did her best to stay strong, to believe that it would all work out for them.

She took a deep breath, switched off the television and placed her unfinished hot chocolate on the table.

'Okay, Angela, bring on the trakehner!' she said, casting her anxieties aside. 'Let's practise right now.'

'That's the spirit!' said Angela.

The trakehner Duncan had built wasn't nearly as large as the one Livvy James had tackled, but it was still daunting for a young rider like Tilly. Magic was only hesitant because Tilly took her legs off and allowed him to look down into the ditch.

'He's only bothered because he can sense that you are,' Angela explained. 'Over-riding it from too far out will make him suspicious. Show him you're confident, then he'll trust you. I know trakehners look frightening, but really they are one of the more straightforward fences. Don't focus on the ditch. Focus on the timber, just as you would with a normal fence. Sit up, eyes up, ride forward and take it in your stride.'

Tilly shortened her reins, gave Magic a nudge with her heels, and picked up a good energetic canter. When they approached the jump, they added a little speed and went at it straight. Despite Angela's advice, as the ditch loomed Tilly felt her gaze drawn to the hollow beneath the log. As soon as she looked down, so did Magic, which made him put in a rather awkward jump.

Tilly groaned with frustration.

'I told you not to drop your focus!' insisted Angela. 'When you look down, you simply pitch your weight forward. You have to sit up and keep him more forward without over-riding and chasing him at the fence.'

'Okay,' said Tilly. 'Okay.'

Determined to overcome this, she gave Magic an encouraging kick with both legs, then took him round a second time. She fixed her eyes on a tree in the distance, so that she wouldn't be tempted to look at the ditch. She urged Magic forwards, willing him to be the bold, brave horse she knew he could be, and willing herself to be just as bold and brave. This time she kept him in a much more positive rhythm, picturing the way Livvy rode. Magic cleared the fence with ease, and landed cleanly on the other side.

'As effortless as Livvy James!' said Angela, smiling.

'Good boy!' said Tilly, patting Magic's neck. 'I knew we could do it more confidently.'

Magic shook his head triumphantly as he did joyful little mini-bucks. He always knew when Tilly was pleased with him. He bobbed his head then they trotted back to Angela.

'That was much better. A lot more confident.

If you jump like that at the weekend, then I'd say you'll get picked –'

'Picked for what?' said a voice behind them.

Tilly swung round. It was her brother, Brook, approaching the fence and waving.

'Hi!' she said.

'Hello, Brook,' said Angela.

He leaned heavily on his walking stick. Even though it had been some time since his riding accident, he still relied on it.

'You're looking well,' said Angela, trying to cover her concern.

'Yeah, feeling well,' said Brook. 'I love this time of year.'

He smiled up at the canopy of golden-brown leaves and the blue, blustery autumn sky.

'It's so nice to be outside. I'm fed up of the four walls of that physiotherapy room. Dad drove me over for some fresh air. I've just paid a visit to Solo, so I thought I'd come and check on my favourite sister's training progress. What is it you're hoping to get picked for?'

Tilly smiled.

'Um, the Junior Regional Team for the Championships at Weston Park – hopefully.'

It pained her to say it.

She knew Brook had had his heart set on the Championships. For ages they'd talked about how it was his big chance to shine. And then it had all been snatched away from him.

The horror of it came back to Tilly in flashes – dreadful images of Solo spooking while hacking on the road, of Brook losing his seat, then being flung to the ground. The sounds of screeching brakes, neighing, shouting and sirens – Tilly knew them only too well, because she'd heard the whole disaster on her phone. To make matters worse, she'd been abroad at the time, grooming for Livvy James at Luhmühlen.

Listening to the trauma, hundreds of miles away, she'd never felt so helpless in her life.

Now, Brook was finally walking again and Solo, his horse, was making progress. Solo had sustained a leg injury that had nearly ended his life, but thankfully, with great vet care, he'd pulled through. Keen to help, Angela had suggested Silver Shoe Farm take Solo on as a companion horse for some of the farm regulars such as Red Admiral and Pride and Joy. That way, Brook and Solo could still spend plenty of time together during their long rehabilitation.

'Weston Park!' said Brook encouragingly. 'Come on, Tilly. You know you'll get picked. You've had such a good season.'

'Yes,' she said, casting her eyes down. 'It's just –'

'Just what?'

'I wish – you *know* what I wish.'

Brook smiled and flicked his hair back. He'd

let it grow since the accident.

'Don't worry about me. I'm fine. I'm on my feet again and, yes, it is frustrating that I'm missing out on some competitions but it's all looking positive for the future. I'll just have to learn how to be patient, give myself and Solo all the time that's needed so that when we make our return we're one hundred per cent ready.'

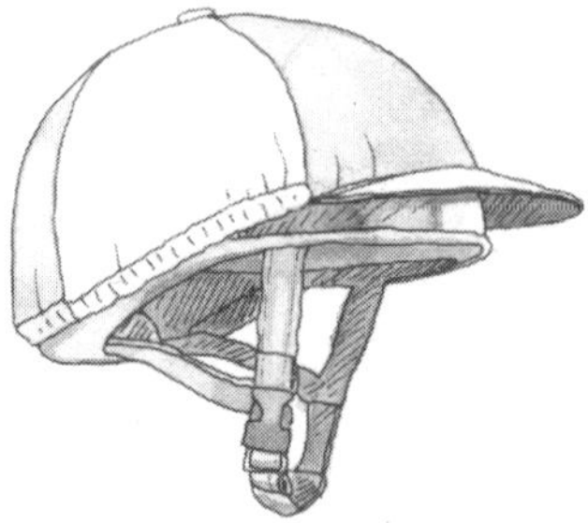

Two

The event was busy despite the wind and rain. The sea of raincoats and umbrellas was distracting for some of the less experienced horses, but Magic knew what was expected of him. Having completed what to him were the two serious phases, the dressage and show jumping, his mind was now absorbed by the prospect of the fun phase, the cross-country.

'We're due to go soon,' whispered Tilly, as she checked his tack was correctly in place. 'Do me proud!'

She walked him down towards the warm-up area for the cross-country, meeting her friends, Anna and Ben, who were returning from the course with their horses, Matinee and Hedgehunter. All four of them were splattered in mud.

'How did you get on?' asked Tilly.

'Wow! It's sloppy out there!' said Anna.

'Yeah,' said Ben. 'The ground is totally churned up after the sixth fence. Be careful, won't you?'

'Wasn't my best round,' Anna went on, 'which is gutting, because I think I caught a glimpse of one of the selectors.'

'Hey, don't worry, they'll take the weather conditions into account,' said Ben. 'I mean, it looks like everyone's having to ride sensibly in the difficult muddy ground.'

He nodded towards another couple of mud-splattered riders, who were moaning about their large amount of time penalties.

'Uh oh,' said Tilly anxiously. 'This could be tricky.'

Even though Magic, with all his honesty and spirit, was happy to compete in any weather, she knew a rain-drenched course wouldn't allow for a selector-impressing ride. Nonetheless, she had to do her best in the circumstances. That was all she could do.

'Look, here comes Kya!' said Ben.

The three friends turned to see Kya Mackensie marching towards them. As Ben and Anna waved her over, Tilly felt that familiar sense of unease. Despite being her Junior Squad teammate, Tilly, as much as she tried, struggled to class Kya as a friend. Tilly knew she had to quietly ignore any unnecessary comments that Kya could make, so that they could get on civilly whenever they were together.

Kya removed her crash helmet and shook out her ice-blonde bob.

'How was it for you?' said Ben. 'You look slightly cleaner than the rest of us!'

Kya shrugged.

'We were brilliant,' she said. 'Bastion isn't bothered by a spot of mud.'

'Did you see any of the selectors?' said Anna.

'Of course. There were three of them at the finish line when I came in. They acknowledged me as I walked past them on my way back to the horsebox.'

'Cool.'

'Yeah, cool,' said Tilly, with a courteous smile.

'Isn't it? I'm so glad I've got through to the Champs.'

Tilly blinked.

'How do you know?' she said. 'They haven't chosen yet.'

Kya grinned.

'I really shouldn't tell anyone this,' she

whispered, 'but, actually, my mum had a conversation with the chairman last week, who secretly told her I'm already the favourite.'

As she said this, she shifted her gaze sideways to Tilly, as if she wanted a reaction. Tilly, determined not to give one, started twiddling her horsehair bracelets.

'Anyway,' said Kya smartly, 'the other big news is that I'm getting a sponsor.'

There was a chorus of gasps. Tilly resisted rolling her eyes.

'Well, with the way things are going,' said Kya, glancing in Tilly's direction again, 'it's more than likely I'll be asked to compete in my first European Championships next year. My dad says he'll finance one foreign trip, but if I'm asked to do more – which I know I will be – he says I'll need to get funding.'

'Definitely,' said Ben. 'Foreign competitions cost a fortune.'

'And if you get a sponsor,' said Anna, 'it'll massively raise your profile. Not to mention the fact that you might get loads of freebies!'

'I know,' said Kya smugly. 'That's why we're targeting some of the coolest clothing brands. My dad's also suggested I could model for them. You know, like be the new face for one of the major brands.'

Tilly wasn't going to dwell on the fact that Kya could model and be cool and get sponsored as the prettiest, smartest, best young rider in the whole wide world . . . She had more important things to think about.

'Excuse me,' she said, shortening up Magic's reins. 'I'd love to chat, but I've got to warm up for the cross-country. I go soon. Come on, boy!' she said, fixing her sights on the entrance to the cross-country warm-up.

As she rode away she felt pleased with herself for rising above Kya's bragging, and that she was able to keep quiet, which clearly annoyed Kya. She heard Kya whispering to the others, 'What's up with *her*? Why's she always so moody? You'd have thought she'd at least be pleased for me.'

The drizzle dampened Tilly's face as she set off from the start. She was wet through before she even started her round, but she would rather that than wear a bulky raincoat over her body protector. The rain didn't bother Magic at all. He felt sturdy and sure-footed, thanks to the large studs that Tilly had screwed into his shoes, and was as keen as ever to get to the first fence. Tilly, however, started a little more slowly than usual. Since Brook's accident, safety was uppermost in her mind.

Soon enough the first jumps came into view – a straightforward log, an angled house followed by a couple of step-downs, which then led into a tricky narrow brush. Magic cleared them neatly. Next up: the trakehner.

'Eyes up!' Tilly told herself, remembering Angela's advice.

As they approached the obstacle, Tilly sensed a blur of faces flanking the course, waving and cheering her on. Was one of them a Regional selector? Without knowing for sure, she found her line and bravely rode Magic towards the trakehner, her concentration now completely on the daunting fence in front of her.

'Please get over this jump,' she whispered. 'Just keep looking up and beyond.'

Brook's accident, Fred Webb, Weston Championships, even Kya and her sponsorship deal – all became insignificant in the moments leading up to the jump. Everything fell into place: great rhythm, perfect stride and a spectacular jump.

'Good boy!' cried Tilly, as she accelerated away from the dreaded fence. 'Magic, you're the best!'

The rest of the round rode well, despite the drizzle turning into a downpour, Tilly and Magic reached the finish in a very respectable time considering the conditions, securing the win – a fraction ahead of Kya. They'd done all they could. Now it was simply a matter of waiting to see if they had been selected to represent the region, assuming that what Kya had said about already being chosen wasn't true.

That evening, Tilly's parents rewarded her efforts with takeaway pizza and ice cream. They sat together in the kitchen, with the radio playing in the background as they ate.

'So, I was talking to Kya's mother at the event,' said Tilly's mum, between mouthfuls. 'She was telling me about Kya's plans to find a sponsor. Sounds great.'

'Yeah, great,' said Tilly, unable to mask her sarcasm.

Her parents exchanged looks.

'Your mum and I have been having a bit of a think,' her dad said.

Tilly sensed the conversation might be taking an ominous turn.

'About what?'

'About how much money we can keep putting into your riding.'

Tilly's heart sank.

'It's not that we don't want to, Tiger Lil', but it's getting beyond our means. We can't afford to keep sending you to competitions. The entry fees alone are a fortune, not to mention the travel expenses and stable fees. Angela's been fantastic, lending us equipment, giving

Magic free livery. And you've certainly worked hard to earn it. But now that you're heading for the next level –'

'What we're saying,' said Tilly's mum, 'before you start to panic, is that we think you should try to find a sponsor too.'

Tilly shrugged.

'Well, obviously I'd LOVE to find a sponsor, but . . . '

She stood up, overwhelmed by frustration.

'But I'm not Kya Mackensie! I haven't got model looks, or –'

'No,' her dad interrupted. 'You're not Kya. You're Tilly Redbrow. And you're just as deserving.'

He meant well, but it didn't help. Tilly simply felt belittled by all the snide remarks Kya had ever made, and there had been plenty, about her being an eventing fraud, riding a 'stolen' horse, and being too poor to ride.

'I don't even have a horse!' she exclaimed, close to tears. 'Magic isn't mine, is he?'

Tilly's mum looked down.

'Well, that's another thing we wanted to talk to you about,' she said quietly.

She went to the kitchen sideboard, picked up a letter and passed it to Tilly. It was official-looking. The logo at the top said Brim and Gloucester Solicitors Ltd.

'Sorry, Tiger Lil',' said her dad. 'It sounds like Fred Webb is getting a solicitor involved.'

Tilly scanned the letter and felt her heart turn to ice. It said that their client, Fred Webb, had all the necessary paperwork to prove ownership of Magic and would be taking steps to claim his property in due course.

Why? It wasn't fair! Why was *everything* going wrong?

Three

In the middle of the night, Tilly sat up in bed. She'd hardly slept for tossing and turning and fretting about Magic. She pulled on a dressing gown and slippers and crept downstairs to the moonlit living room, where she switched on her little brother Adam's laptop. It had been his Christmas present. He'd asked for a laptop, while Tilly, as usual, had asked for more riding paraphernalia: a new jacket, a soft leather bridle for Magic, vouchers for her favourite riding shops. Despite all the fads and phases Adam had been through

– football, wrestling, athletics, and now, computers – Tilly had only ever set her sights on one thing: horses.

She clicked on the internet icon and started searching through the myriad of equestrian company websites. Surely one of them would be interested in sponsoring a girl like her? All the top riders had sponsors. They relied on them for funding and supplies of equipment. But that was the point, thought Tilly. *Top riders.*

Apart from being mentioned in a few articles in the local papers, Tilly and Magic were nobodies. Who'd be interested in them? Especially when their future together was so uncertain. Nonetheless, she steeled herself and started to write out a list of companies she liked the sound of, ranging from traditional clothing to fashion clothing to tack and feed and veterinary supplies. If Kya was planning to get a sponsor, then she had to as well.

Once her list was complete, she started planning a letter:

> Dear Sir/Madam,
>
> My name is Tilly Redbrow. I'm an ambitious young event rider, competing at novice level. This year I was selected for Junior Squad training. You may not have heard of me yet, but one day, I hope to be among the best in the country. This is all thanks to my incredible grey, Magic Spirit. Let me tell you about Magic. He's not your average horse. He's not a thoroughbred sired from a world-famous stud. In fact, his background is a bit of a mystery and sometimes he can be a bit tricky with people he doesn't know. But I need to tell you that he's AMAZING. It all started in my village, North Cosford. I was driving with my mum and we came across this commotion: it was an agitated loose horse. He looked frightened and thin. He wouldn't let anyone come near him. And then . . .

It was too much. Tilly couldn't continue. Just thinking about the moment she met Magic made her tearful. What had Fred Webb done to that poor horse to make him so distressed? If Fred hadn't cared for him then, he obviously wasn't going to care for him now. She shut down the computer, wiped her tears and sloped back to bed.

Tilly was woken early by a message. Bleary-eyed, she checked her phone:

Fancy a pre-breakfast hack? Meet you at the entrance to Silver Shoe in half an hour? H x

It was from Harry Grey, one of the few people who could cheer her up. They'd met and ridden together on the Junior Squad and had gradually grown closer. Tilly didn't dare use the word 'boyfriend', but secretly she liked the idea. Harry was funny and kind, but more importantly, he was passionate about eventing. He understood Tilly's hopes and dreams, because his were similar. His powerful liver chestnut, Nobleman, was a genuine trier, an all rounder with a huge, scopey jump.

Even though Tilly was tired and glum, she was pleased about his invitation. She didn't have a lot of time because after mucking out, feeding and yard duties, she had to get to school, but she was determined to squeeze in a hack with Harry and Nobleman. She quickly sent a reply then jumped in the shower, hoping her mum would be willing to drop her at Silver Shoe Farm early.

Within twenty-five minutes, Tilly was at the yard, pulling on her boots, zipping up her fleece and grabbing a broom. The mornings were getting colder. The warm haze of summer had faded. Magic's breath twisted from his nostrils in a stream of vapour. He bobbed his head as Tilly came near.

'Morning, boy! Did you have a good night? Not too chilly? We'll have to get your winter rug out soon.'

She yawned. Magic pricked his ears.

'Sorry. Didn't mean to startle you . . . I'm just super-tired. Not that you need to worry, but you, beautiful boy, are causing me so much heartache.'

She held his face and hugged him.

'I'll never hold it against you. Fancy a hack with Harry and Nobleman?'

Magic whickered.

'Well, let's give you a quick brush and get your tack on. I'm afraid you'll have to wait till we're back for your breakfast.'

Harry and Nobleman were waiting at the gate. As soon as Harry saw Tilly, his face lit up with a warm smile. She liked his teeth and the cute dimples in his cheeks. He looked boyish and grown-up at the same time.

'Morning!'

'G'morning!'

The two horses greeted one another with low muffled whickers.

'Horses are so random!' laughed Harry. 'Shall we go?'

'Yes.'

Tilly gave Magic a nudge, but couldn't stifle another big yawn.

'Have I bored you already?' said Harry.

'Oh, no. I'm just tired today. Didn't sleep very well.'

'Me neither. I kept thinking about the selection. You know they're announcing the team for Weston today –'

'I know,' said Tilly tensely.

Harry paused, looked at her.

'It's not just that, is it?'

Tilly sighed.

'You can talk to me about it,' said Harry. 'I want to help. I know you like to tell your woes to Magic, but let's face it, he's not very good at giving advice, is he?'

'No,' answered Tilly, smiling, ' he is a good listener though.'

They walked down the lane, through the puddles, avoiding the potholes. Golden leaves fluttered all around them and the hedgerows were thick with berries. Piece by piece, Tilly shared her worries about Magic and Fred Webb and sponsorship and desperately wanting to get through to compete at Weston Park, for Brook's sake.

'You certainly know how to pile the pressure on yourself,' said Harry.

He pulled off onto a farm track. Tilly and Magic followed. The track led them steeply uphill to a magnificent oak tree. They lingered there for a moment.

'We should get off,' said Harry, swinging his leg over Nobleman's back.

'Why?' asked Tilly.

He came round and took her hand, then looked into her eyes and smiled.

'Because I think you need a hug . . . and I can't hug you while you're on your horse.'

Tilly blushed. Her stomach filled with butterflies. She dismounted and shyly faced Harry. Magic stood beside her, his kind, dark eyes twinkling. Then Harry, still holding Nobleman's reins, put his arms around Tilly and held her close. It wasn't as if they hadn't hugged before to celebrate competition victories and training successes. But this was different. At competitions they were surrounded by others, part of a group. Now it was just the two of them, with Magic and Nobleman, by the oak tree.

'I've got a feeling,' whispered Harry, gazing into Tilly's eyes. 'A feeling that everything's going to work out for you. Chin up. Keep going.'

He leaned forward and kissed her forehead, then held his lips against her skin. He ran his hands down the twists of her plaits. Tilly closed her eyes. She could feel her heart racing, the flutter in her stomach overwhelming everything. The longer Harry held the kiss, the more amazing it felt. For the first time in ages, she felt hopeful and strong.

'Thank you,' she whispered.

'Okay,' said Harry, breaking away. 'Enough mushy stuff! Now let's do what we do best. We'll go back across the fields to Silver Shoe. Come on, race you back!'

'You're on! ' said Tilly, eyes as bright as Magic's.

They remounted and accelerated across the fields. Magic and Nobleman delighted in the chance to stretch out their legs and go full pelt. They didn't stop until they reached Silver Shoe. Tilly felt exhilarated and free and happy, and of course, even though Harry gave it his best effort, it was her who got to the gate first.

Four

'What's with you today?' said Tilly's best friend, Becky.

They were sitting at the back of the biology lab, trying to spot amoebas through a microscope.

'It's as though you're in another zone.'

Becky clicked her fingers at Tilly, but Tilly simply rested her chin on her hand and sighed.

'Seriously,' said Becky. 'Earth to Planet Pony!'

'Stuff on my mind,' protested Tilly. 'I'm waiting for a phone call to see whether I've been selected for the Regional Team – you know, for the Under 18 Championships.'

'But that normally makes you tense and panicky. Not day-dreamy.'

'Okay. So, maybe there's something else . . .'

'What?'

Tilly closed her eyes.

'He's *so nice*,' she whispered, smiling to herself.

'Who?'

'Harry Grey.'

'You mean the riding boy you've been going on and on about? The Junior Squad one? Tell me! What's happened?'

'We hugged and . . . kissed . . . sort of.'

Becky clapped her hands and squealed.

'How? When?'

They both started giggling – until Mr Wilson, the biology teacher, marched over to their desk.

'Girls! This isn't a social club. Honestly,

what's all the fuss about?'

'Nothing, Mr Wilson,' said Tilly.

'We're just talking about biology,' said Becky, innocently.

For the rest of the day, Tilly was distracted by a muddle of happy thoughts about Harry and anxious thoughts about being selected for Weston and keeping Magic. She couldn't wait to get to her evening training session, where she could focus totally on her riding. The squad – including Harry – were having an informal show jump practice at Silver Shoe.

Midway there, in the passenger seat of her dad's car, Tilly's phone started to buzz. She glanced at it, then back at her dad.

'Well, answer it,' he said. 'It's the only way you'll find out.'

Tilly gulped and pressed accept.

'Tilly?' said a voice. 'It's Ginny Henderson from British Eventing.'

'Hi,' said Tilly, nervously.

'Well, I won't keep you guessing. The news you want to hear is that you're in.'

'I am?'

Tilly nearly dropped the phone.

'Of course.'

Tilly screamed. Her dad winced at the noise, then smiled and gave her a thumbs-up.

'You've had a great season,' said Ginny. 'And we've all been impressed by the way you've handled some of the stresses you've been through this year. You've shown bravery and guts. But on that note, I have to warn you that the place is conditional.'

'Conditional? On what?'

'We understand that the ownership of your horse is currently being contested –'

Tilly's heart sank.

'Well, yes, but –'

'You understand that it's you and Magic Spirit as a combination that we're interested in. If it turns out that Magic Spirit is no longer available for you to ride, then you'll have to withdraw. I'm sorry.'

Tilly shuddered.

'Obviously, if it works out in your favour and the matter can be resolved *before* the competition –'

'Yes,' said Tilly. 'I'll do my best.'

'Luckily we have Kya Mackensie and Bastion as our reserve combination. It was tight between you two, but we really want to give you this chance, Tilly.'

'Of course,' said Tilly, suddenly numb.

Tilly waved goodbye to her dad, fetched a saddle and bridle from the tack room, then collected Magic from the paddock. She had an apple in her pocket. She held it out and he came straight to the fence. He crunched eagerly, as she stood in a daze, wishing she could miraculously find the money to buy Fred Webb out of his stake in Magic. In fact, she'd give him all the money in the world if it meant she could keep her dream horse by her side.

'Well, boy, we've made it through to Weston Park,' she whispered. 'Now we've got to hope and pray that we can stay together.'

Just then a familiar horse trotted up to join them. It was Solo.

'Hello, Solo!' Tilly called. 'How are you?'

She gave Solo a hug. He prodded her affectionately with his nose and bothered her for an apple.

'Sorry. I only brought one. Next time, I'll remember a treat for you too. I promise.'

Her eyes slipped to the scar on his front leg. His injury had healed well, but the sight of it triggered memories of Brook's accident.

'I was telling Magic how we've got through to Weston Park,' she whispered. 'I wish you and Brook were doing it too. Maybe next year.'

She stroked Solo's nose. The sadness welled inside her, until she was distracted by a message from Harry:

We're at the sand school, about to start. Where are you? Any news on Weston Park? I'm in, but Kya's fuming because she's only a reserve! H x

Tilly replied:

Just about to tack up. Be there in 5. And, yes, I'm in . . . just! Know anyone with lots of money to spare?! Need to buy my horse urgently x

She said goodbye to Solo, placed Magic's saddle on his back, tightened the girth, and led him up the path to the sand school.

'Hey, Tilly,' said Ben.

'Hiya,' said Anna. 'Well done on getting into the Championships – Harry told us. Ben and I didn't get in, but we've not been going that well recently, so we weren't expecting to. You've been really consistent all season though, Tilly. You totally deserve your place.'

'Thanks,' said Tilly, touched that Anna was being so supportive.

In the distance, she could see Kya and Bastion furiously cantering in circles. Bastion's coat was shining and he was wearing a glittery bridle – another new piece of tack for his vast collection.

'She isn't happy,' whispered Ben. 'I'd steer clear if I were you.'

Tilly nodded.

Harry came behind, dragging a pole.

'Hey, you made it,' he said, breaking into a smile. 'Angela's busy, but she suggested we practise some grid work, and concentrate on our own positions. I'll need a hand setting up.'

'I'll help,' said Tilly. 'I'll hold the horses, while you lug the poles. So, what's Angela up to?'

'Oh, she's got visitors,' said Harry.

'You mean the couple that pulled up in that amazing silver 4x4?' said Ben, hoisting the other end of the pole. 'That's some car. Worth a fortune.'

Tilly wondered who he meant. She'd been at Silver Shoe long enough to know the different faces who came and went. It was unlikely to be new customers. Angela's livery was full, as usual.

'Can't you all hurry up!' Kya snapped from the other side of the school. 'I mean, how long does it take to put up a few jumps?'

'You could help,' said Ben.

Kya just huffed.

When the row of fences was finally in place, they took turns popping up the grid, observing and giving feedback on each other's techniques. When it came to Tilly's turn, Ben, Anna and Harry were complimentary.

'So straight!'

'Good position, your leg looked secure!'

Kya, however, managed to find faults that weren't even there.

'Do you know you pull a silly face every time you take off?' she said. 'You should be careful. If you get caught on camera like that, it could be embarrassing.'

'Like it matters?' said Harry, defensively. 'It's not a silly face anyway. It's a look of determination.'

He caught Tilly's eye and smiled.

'Whatever,' said Kya. 'Determination doesn't buy horses. Money does.'

Tilly tensed.

'Don't respond,' whispered Harry. 'Don't lower yourself. She's just jealous and trying to wind you up.'

Taking his advice, Tilly nudged Magic forwards and circled the sand school, counting in her head to calm herself down. Meanwhile, Kya announced she was leaving early.

'Actually, I've got to get to a photo shoot,' she said, making sure Tilly could hear. 'Kelston Equestrian is interested in getting me to front their teen riding campaign. They're about to become the most fashionable new clothing brand out there. Look at this beautiful bridle with a sparkly browband they sent for Bastion.'

She pulled Bastion's reins. He waved his head, as though he wanted everyone to see his sparkly tack. *Like horse, like rider*, thought Tilly.

'They've offered me loads of free stuff: rugs, boots, breeches, you name it – everything I need for competitions. They've also said they can't wait to develop a long-term partnership with me. Their Head of Marketing told my dad that he thinks Bastion and I are ideal role models for their brand. Honestly, it's a dream come true. We won't have to worry about a thing.'

With that, she flicked her hair and trotted out of the gate.

'It's so sad that Kya feels she has to prove a point the whole time,' said Anna.

'Yes, she always has to make out that she's better than everyone else,' said Ben.

'Actually, I think she's the opposite and quite insecure, and that's why she puts on a front,' said Tilly.

'You might be right,' said Harry, nodding. 'That's why I try my hardest not to let it bother me, because deep down I don't think she means it. Thank you for sticking up for me though. It means a lot,' said Tilly.

Horses are great, she thought, *but sometimes, just sometimes, human friends are even better.*

Five

As Tilly left Silver Shoe that evening, sure enough, she caught sight of Angela's mystery visitors. They were standing in front of their gleaming silver car talking with Angela and Duncan – a well-dressed middle-aged couple, wearing matching green waxed jackets. The woman had brown wavy hair and the man had a grey beard. Tilly didn't recognise them, but she was struck by the way they were chatting warmly, like the oldest of friends.

Tilly didn't want to interrupt, but as she

passed, they stopped talking. Angela waved at her. The couple smiled, so Tilly smiled back, then realised she had an embarrassing clump of straw stuck to her boot, so hurried away to the tack room.

Later that evening after supper, she phoned Brook to see how he was doing.

'I saw Solo today,' she said. 'He was grazing with Magic. It was so sweet. He came up to see if I had a treat for him. He's looking so much better.'

'Yeah, I think he really likes being at Silver Shoe,' said Brook. 'I'm glad. So what about Weston Park?'

'We're in,' said Tilly.

'I knew you would be.'

'But,' she closed her eyes, 'only if it works out with Magic. We received a letter from Fred Webb's solicitor the other day. Fred's planning to take him back. And if he takes him before the competition, then it's over for me and Magic and our places will be given to – ugh – Kya and Bastion!'

'Not Kya!'

'Oh, Brook, it's so tough! Everything seems to be going against me! Even if I do get to keep riding Magic, my parents are worrying about the cost of competitions. I just want to do what I love, but there are so many expenses: feed, tack, entry fees, transport, stabling costs . . . I don't know what to do.'

'Don't get upset, ' said Brook. 'Funnily enough, I was talking to my mum about what we should do with our horsebox. Solo won't be travelling for a while so if it helps, you can have it. Then you won't need to keep borrowing or hiring from other people. I know it's not everything, but it will make life a bit easier, won't it?'

'Oh, Brook, you're the loveliest big brother in the world! Thank you!'

'Just one condition –'

Tilly looked up.

'You make sure you win!'

Tilly threw her head back and smiled.

'No pressure, then?'

In the weeks leading up to Weston Park, there was no further news from Fred Webb or his solicitor. Secretly, Tilly was surprised but hoped he was losing interest and focused her attention on training. She also tried to avoid Kya as much as possible. She didn't want anything – especially Kya's rather negative attitude – distracting her from what mattered.

She and Magic went through sequence after sequence of dressage, perfecting every movement – square halts, rein-backs, walks, trots, extended trots and collected canters. She practised jumps of different kinds, both in the arena and cross-country. And with

Angela's guidance, plus a few more viewings of Livvy James' Bramham footage.

At the end of one of these intense jumping sessions, a week before the competition itself, Tilly sponged Magic down and gave him a mint.

'Good work, boy!' she said, rewarding him with a pat. 'You've worked so hard. You know, I don't want to jinx it, but I'm finally getting a good feeling about this, like Harry said. I mean, we're in the best shape ever. Thanks to Brook, we've got our own horsebox. And, for now, no one seems to be trying to take you away from me –'

She held her breath as she said this and crossed her fingers. Then her phone beeped. She jumped. Thankfully, it was Harry.

'Hi,' she said brightly.

'Hiya, Tilly.'

He sounded bothered.

'What's up?'

'You're not going to believe this . . . Nobleman and I aren't going to make it to Weston Park.'

'Oh no! Why not?'

'He was rolling around before his bath last night. He must have knocked his knee. It's swollen. I don't think it's anything serious, but he's had problems with it before. We don't want to take any chances. He's had a great season. I think it's time to call it quits for this year.'

'Of course,' said Tilly. 'Best not to push it, but what a shame!'

'We're okay. It's how it goes sometimes. Although, you know what this means for you?'

Tilly blinked.

'My replacement on the team,' said Harry. 'It's *you know who.*'

Tilly groaned.

'That's right. You don't have to worry about Kya taking your place any more – because now you're going head to head with her!'

'Tilly clasped her hand to her forehead.

'Help!' she said.

'We'll all be rooting for you,' he said, then after a pause, 'especially me.'

So, thought Tilly, as she led Magic back to the yard, *the competition was on!* She tried to imagine what was going through Kya's head. Was she thinking about how she could get the best out of herself and Bastion, or was she planning their fancy Kelston Equestrian outfits and working out how many different ways she could put Tilly and Magic down?

'It doesn't matter what she's thinking,' she muttered, half smiling, taking Magic's reins. 'We'll just concentrate on our own performance, won't we, boy?' As they neared the turning into the yard, however, Tilly heard raised voices. She slowed and stopped, worried the noise would agitate Magic. She could hear Duncan. He was arguing, which was very unlike him. Tilly crept a little closer and surveyed the scene. She saw a horsebox parked across the gate.

Duncan stood in front of the driver's door.

'Go!' he was shouting. 'Get out of here before I call the police!'

Whoever was in the vehicle obviously wasn't welcome.

Magic side-stepped and pushed back his ears. He could sense something wasn't right – and so could Tilly.

'It's okay, boy,' she whispered, holding him tightly, but as she spoke, a strange chill rippled through her legs and arms. Her chest started to feel tight. The hairs on her neck stood up.

She knew what was going on, why Duncan was so cross.

He'd come.

Fred Webb had finally come for Magic.

Frozen, Tilly watched as Angela came out of the clubhouse, her red hair flaming behind her. She too raised her voice and asked him to leave, pointing towards the exit gate. Tilly stared at the windscreen. She could just about make out the face behind the steering wheel: heavy jowls, a bulbous red nose, grey bushy brows and small, mean eyes.

Despite Duncan and Angela's protests, Fred Webb got out of the car. He started shouting over them, his fat belly hanging over his jeans. He had papers in his hands, which he waved angrily in Angela's face. The fact that he'd brought his horsebox with him showed his intention. Tilly gasped at the thought of Magic being taken away in that dilapidated box – it wasn't road worthy. It wasn't *safe*.

She had to do something. And fast. Her mind raced. She looked at the yard, then back at the fields behind her. There was a lane at the end, which led onto the road. If she could get to it in time . . .

Without questioning the idea, she shoved her foot into the stirrup, swung into the saddle and pulled Magic round. In tune with her fear, Magic threw his head back and set off at lightning speed. He also let out a loud, anxious whinny. Tilly had a second to look back and see that the whinny had caught everyone's attention. They'd been spotted. Angela and Duncan looked over with alarm. So did Fred.

'There he is!' Fred shouted. 'There's the nag! I told you! Get him for me! *Now!*'

Suddenly, all three of them, Angela, Duncan and Fred, started running over. Tilly kicked hard. Magic picked up the pace. His hooves flew over the ground as if he was racing for his life. Angela called Tilly's name, cried out for her to stop, but Tilly chose not to.

She chose to keep going.

She *had* to keep going.

Six

With the wind whipping the leaves around them, Tilly and Magic raced across the fields, over the brow of the hill towards the back lane. They soon lost sight of Fred and the others, but they carried on going. It wasn't until they reached the old oak tree at the top of the next hill that they finally slowed.

They came to a standstill at the exact spot where Tilly and Harry had hugged weeks before, on that lovely early morning hack. Tilly had been so happy in that moment. She wished she had Harry with her right now.

Her heart was pounding. Her legs felt like jelly. She glanced back across the valley, but there was no sign of anyone. As soon as she caught her breath, she dismounted and gave Magic a pat. His coat was shining with sweat. He'd worked hard to cover that ground. He stared at her with his dark, soulful eyes.

She stroked his nose and held him close.

'I won't let anything happen to you, boy, I promise. I won't let him take you.'

Magic closed his eyes. A golden oak leaf fluttered and landed between his ears. He twitched. Tilly picked it off and held it out.

'The seasons can change all they want,' she said defiantly, as she stared at the leaf, 'but you and I won't change. We're meant to be together. I know we are. Even if it means we have to run away forever.'

She threw her arms around Magic's neck and leaned against his warm shoulder. He bowed his head and snorted.

'Where shall we go?' she whispered, more to herself than to Magic.

She had no food or drink. Magic could make do with grass and water from streams, but it wouldn't be long before she was hungry and thirsty. It was cold too. Her fleece and jodhpurs were fine for the day, but not the night. And more importantly, Magic had no rug. She didn't want him catching a chill.

Her mind started to whirl.

Should she ring her parents? Should she tell them she was running away with Magic? She didn't want them to worry. Should she tell Brook? Or Harry? Should she try to find a stable yard in the next town and ask them to keep quiet about her arrival? Should she head for the woods? Or the coast? Magic was already hot and tired. Should she keep him running, keep him going until . . . until . . .

'Tilly?'

A voice sailed up from the bottom of the hill.

Tilly froze.

It was Angela.

'Are you up there, Tilly?'

By the way Angela was calling, Tilly could tell she hadn't spotted her yet. She'd obviously seen the direction they'd galloped off in and had followed. What now? Should Tilly make herself known, or run? She knew that Angela, of all people, was on her side, but she felt scared.

'Tilly! Come out! Don't be frightened! We'll sort this out!'

Magic whickered and bobbed his head. Tilly clutched his reins. She could hear hoof-beats on the hill. Angela was riding, most likely her favourite horse, Pride and Joy. There was no point trying to outrun a powerful horse like him.

Tilly glanced at Magic, then back to the hill.

'Now or never,' she whispered to herself, her heart thumping so hard it felt as though it was going to burst out of her. 'Now or never.'

She jumped into the saddle. She gripped the reins and tucked her feet into the stirrups. She prepared to gallop, but –

She couldn't do it.

With trembling hands and wide eyes, she waited.

Seconds later, Angela came over the hill, bareback on Pride and Joy.

'There you are!' said Angela, her face softening with relief. 'Oh, Tilly!'

Tilly burst into tears.

Angela walked Pride and Joy forwards. He greeted Magic with a nod. The two horses stood obediently side by side, while Angela gave Tilly a hug.'I know how cruel and unfair it feels,' said Angela, as they began the walk back to the farmhouse. 'But we can't break the law.'

Tilly sniffed and nodded.

'We'll find a solution eventually, but for

now, we have to let Mr Webb take ownership of Magic. He has Magic's passport and the paperwork in place. And he's determined. All in all, he doesn't seem like a very reasonable man. The moment he came into the yard he started yelling and cursing.'

'That's what I'm worried about,' said Tilly. 'If I thought Magic would be going somewhere where he'd be loved and cared for, it might be a bit easier, but . . . Fred Webb isn't a nice person!'

Angela sighed, leaned sideways and squeezed Tilly's hand.

'I know. I *know*.'

As they neared the farmhouse, Tilly could feel Magic's pace slowing. It was as if he knew what was coming.

'It's okay, boy,' she said, fighting tears. 'Don't be afraid.'

They led their horses along the drive, then through the gate and around the barns. Fred

Webb was leaning on his dirty silver jeep, talking loudly into his phone. The sight of him made Tilly angry. Sensing her tension, Magic grew agitated. As they entered the yard, he stomped sideways and repeatedly threw up his head. When Fred Webb turned to face him, he let out an unusual but ferocious-sounding whinny.

Tilly did nothing to control Magic's outburst. She was glad he was misbehaving.

'That's it, boy,' she whispered. 'Put him off. Show him your troublesome side. He thinks he should have you – but he doesn't know you like I do!'

Magic whinnied again.

'There you are!' roared Fred Webb. 'So, you're the elusive Tilly Redbrow, then. That was a fine stunt you pulled, running away with someone else's property . . . you're lucky I didn't call the police!'

'Magic isn't property,' said Tilly, snarling.

'He's a living being.'

'Maybe so, but he's *my* living being now!'

Fred gave Magic an over-hard pat on the hindquarters. Magic snorted and kicked out with his hind leg, threateningly.

'Bad-tempered beast, isn't he? I thought he was supposed to be an up and coming competition horse. Come on. Let's load him up then. It's not as though I haven't already wasted enough time.'

'I'll need to check your horsebox first,' said Angela, catching Tilly's eye. 'It's my policy. I never let a horse leave my yard unless I know their transport is road-worthy.'

Fred Webb shrugged. 'Do what you like, but that horse is coming with me.'

Duncan walked over to Tilly. 'Angela will do what she can to delay him,' he whispered, which will give you and Magic a chance to say goodbye.'

'Okay, thanks,' said Tilly.

Gently, she tugged Magic's reins and moved him over to the fence. With her, he was calm and obliging once more. He bowed his head as she tickled his ears. He nudged her shoulder and sniffed her horsehair bracelets just as he'd done when they first met. Tilly told him again and again how much she loved him, then held his face against hers. A single tear rolled down her cheek and onto Magic's nose, but he didn't twitch or shake it away. He just closed his eyes and rested his head on her shoulder.

'Hurry up!' said Fred. 'I told you my horsebox was good.'

'Just about,' said Angela regretfully.

Fred came over to take Magic's reins from Tilly.

'No,' said Tilly. *'I'll* lead him.'

'Suit yourself.'

Steadfast, heart pounding, Tilly walked Magic towards the box. When they reached the black mouth of the entrance, Magic started to pull and rear. Tilly whispered calming sounds as she encouraged him up the ramp. The inside of the box smelled musty, as though it hadn't been used for decades.

'I'm so sorry, boy,' she said. 'Just remember how much I love you.'

She slipped off his bridle, popped on a head collar and tied him up, then hugged him once more. She didn't want to leave him alone, so she stood, stroking his beautiful face. She knew she wasn't going to walk out willingly.

'Right. You've said your goodbyes,' said Fred. 'Time to go. I've got a delivery coming. I don't want to be late.'

'Because a delivery is so much more important than the welfare of a horse,' growled Tilly under her breath.

Magic stomped his hoof.

'Come on, Tilly,' said

Angela, stepping on board and taking her hand. 'Let's go and phone your parents.'

'I don't want to,' said Tilly, panic overtaking her.

Angela looked her in the eye.

'Come on,' she said, in the same firm manner she used with her horses. 'It's time.'

She huddled Tilly away from the horsebox towards the clubhouse.

'Don't look back,' she said, tearful herself now. 'It makes it worse.'

'You'll be okay,' said Duncan, joining them. 'And Magic will be okay too. You know what a brave horse he is.'

Tilly sobbed and nodded. He was brave. One of the bravest.

Seven

After three days, Tilly was still inconsolable. She lay on her bed, clutching her horsehair bracelets – one from Magic's tail, and the one given to her by her biological mother. Aside from Magic himself, they were her most precious things. She also surrounded herself with pictures and newspaper clippings about her competitions with Magic, all their rosettes, and an amazing framed photograph of them leaping over a triple bar at one of last year's Pony Club events. She couldn't eat, even though her mum kept offering her all her favourite treats. She couldn't sleep – every dream involved Magic and made her feel more upset.

'Oh, Tiger Lil',' said her dad, as he came and sat on the end of her bed. 'I can't bear seeing you like this. There must be something we can do to help.'

'I want Magic back,' Tilly sniffed, 'I want to ride.'

'You can still ride,' he said, stroking her hair. 'There are other horses out there. I'm sure Angela will let you exercise some of the horses at Silver Shoe. And you'll find another competition horse soon enough.'

'But I don't want another competition horse! I want Magic!'

Mr Redbrow sighed.

'Maybe I can give Fred Webb a call, arrange for you to visit. His farm isn't too far away from what Angela told me.'

Tilly brightened. She sat up, wiping her eyes.

'Can you?' she said, offering him her phone. 'Please?'

'I can't promise he'll go for it, but it's worth a try.'

Tilly nodded furiously.

'But it doesn't mean we're getting Magic back,' her dad warned her.

'No. But I can at least make sure he's okay and that he's got everything he needs –'

'Come on,' said Tilly's dad. 'I'll call now.'

Tilly held her breath and waited while her dad tapped in Fred Webb's number. It rang and rang.

'He isn't answering. Sorry, Tiger Lil'.'

Tilly sighed.

'Hey, let's do something, shall we?' said her dad. 'We could – I don't know – play mini-golf or something?'

Tilly rolled her eyes.

'Dad, I haven't played mini-golf since I was eight.'

'Okay. Swimming then? We both like swimming.'

'No, thanks. I think I'll stay here. I want to make a memory box of things to do with Magic.'

Her dad nodded, in a somewhat unconvinced way.

Just then, Tilly's phone started buzzing.

'It's him!'

Her dad scooped up the phone, switched on speaker phone and answered.

'Hello, Mr Webb,' he said. 'Thanks for calling back.'

'Well, I was going to call anyway,' said Fred Webb gruffly. 'What exactly has your daughter been doing to that nag? Some competition ride! The animal's wild! Won't let me go near it!'

Tilly couldn't help smiling. Her dad winked at her.

'Sorry to hear that, Mr Webb, but Tilly never had any trouble with Magic. Maybe he's a bit unsettled in his new surroundings.'

'I'll say,' snarled Fred. 'Waste of my time!'

'Maybe we could, er, help?' said Mr Redbrow. 'Tilly would love to visit Magic, and she could always give you some hints on how to handle him while she's there?'

Tilly crossed her fingers. Fred Webb paused as he thought about it, then gave a cough.

'Bit late for that. I'm selling him.'

'What?'

'I've got interest from a dealer in Crewe. Shouldn't take long to sort out.'

Tilly's eyes opened wide.

'NO!'

She knew enough about geography to know that Crewe was at the other end of the country.

'That's miles away! If Magic is taken up there, I'll *never* see him again!'

'Haven't you got other interest?' said her dad, feeling Tilly's panic. 'Someone more local?'

'Well, it hasn't turned out to be the horse I was expecting, has it? Aren't many who'd pay a good price for a disobedient trickster like that!'

Tilly's dad looked angry – Tilly never saw him angry.

'And that's all that matters, is it?' he snapped. 'The amount of money you make? Never mind the welfare of Magic Spirit – or my daughter, for that matter! They had a future together. They were a team! Tilly was the person who could bring the best out in Magic – you should have listened to her. You should have let them stay together.'

Tilly squeezed her dad's arm. She was secretly chuffed that he was speaking so forcefully on her behalf.

'You should be ashamed of yourself,' said

Tilly's dad, glaring into the phone.

'What's done is done,' said Fred Webb. 'Hopefully, that horse will be sold by the weekend. So you might as well accept it and move on.'

He cut the call. Tilly and her dad stared at each other.

'Move on,' said Tilly. 'Does he really think I can just *move on*?'

That afternoon, Harry Grey came over. He brought Tilly a massive bag of her favourite sweets and the latest copy of *Horse and Hound*. She was pleased he'd come, even though she was feeling sad. She knew he'd understand. At first, however, they were both a little bit nervous. They sat on Tilly's bed and talked about what everyone else had been up to.

'Ben's taken his horse on half-term holiday,' said Harry. 'He's in Devon with his parents and they're going to ride on the beach.'

'Nice,' said Tilly, remembering how she'd once ridden a horse called Neptune through the waves in Cornwall.

'And Anna said she might have a break from training and focus on her music stuff instead.'

'Oh. Do you think she's secretly disappointed that she didn't get through to Weston Park?'

'No. Not Anna. She's so laid back, but you know how much she loves her band.'

'Yeah,' said Tilly. 'It's good she's got something else.'

'And Kya's training like crazy – when she's not going on and on about Kelston Equestrian, that is. Honestly, she hasn't shut up. And she's posted tons of pictures of her photo shoot on her social media. Have you seen them?'

'No.'

'Do you want to?'

Tilly sighed. She didn't, but at the same time she had to admit she was intrigued.

'Go on then.'

Harry took out his iPad and loaded the images. There were at least twenty of them, featuring Kya in different poses and outfits against a crisp white background. Some outfits were traditional – jackets, jodhpurs and shirts. Some were cool – padded gilets, fleeces and cute t-shirts. In all of them, Kya looked immaculate. Tilly scrolled through with a heavy heart.

'To be fair, she looks amazing,' she acknowledged.

'Yeah, on the outside,' said Harry, 'but we all know she can be pretty spiteful.'

'I guess,' said Tilly, feeling a pang of envy.

Despite all the mean things Kya said and did, she still seemed to come out on top. She had her horse, her fancy riding equipment, her sponsorship deal. She even had a place at Weston Park, thanks to Harry's misfortune. And what did Tilly have? Anger boiled inside her, and sadness at the loss of her beautiful Magic Spirit.

'You know we're all really upset for you,' said Harry thoughtfully. 'Shall we go for a walk?'

Tilly closed the iPad.

'Yes,' she said. 'I guess it's time I got some fresh air.'

'How strange,' said Harry, as they stepped into the garden. 'You and I are hanging out and, for once, neither of us has a horse at our side!'

'Weird, isn't it?' said Tilly. 'Feels like

something's missing –'

'Yeah, the smell of manure . . . hay . . .'

Tilly laughed.

'How's Nobleman's knee?' she said.

'Good, thanks. The swelling's nearly gone, so I'll probably start him on some light exercise in a few days, but no Weston Park.'

'I guess we're the Weston Park rejects,' said Tilly.

'Yeah. Still, I'd rather have a healthy horse than a chance at a competition.'

'I'd rather have a horse,' said Tilly.

'Of course. Sorry, Tilly, I didn't think. So, is Fred Webb really going to sell Magic? Your dad told me he's got a buyer from Crewe.'

'Sounds like it.'

'That sucks.'

'It really does,' said Tilly, her eyes filling with tears once more.

Without another word, Harry put his arms around her, pressed her face to his chest and hugged her.

Eight

It was as if a big black cloud hung over Silver Shoe Farm. Things weren't the same without Tilly and Magic. Finally, Angela, having spoken to Tilly every day for the past week, convinced her in her no-nonsense way to get down to Silver Shoe.

'No ifs or buts, Tilly. I know you're upset, but there's yard work to be done. I've got a hay delivery that needs shifting and loads of livery horses that want exercising. Your help is necessary. You know the saying, if you fall off a horse, get straight back on –'

'Okay,' said Tilly, not wanting to let Angela down. 'I'll be there as soon as I can.'

Tilly knew it was the right thing to do, but she dreaded seeing Magic's empty stable. She was quietly cheered by the thought of being back in the place she loved, but as her dad drove her along the tree-lined lane, she was haunted by memories. She remembered the first day she'd visited Silver Shoe, her feelings on the drive – an intoxicating mix of joy and anticipation. She recalled the first time she saw Magic in the stable, how frail and timid he'd looked.

At the time, she'd had no idea what an amazing team they would go on to be. But, of course, in a way, she had known. She'd known from the first moment she'd looked into his eyes.

'You all right, Tiger Lil'?' said her dad.

'Yes,' said Tilly. 'Just thinking about good things.'

He smiled at her, in his protective way, then turned through the five-bar gate and parked in the yard.

'What time shall I pick you up?'

Tilly looked at her watch.

'I won't be long,' she said.

'Take all day. Just call when you're done.'

'Thanks, Dad.'

Having been away from Silver Shoe, its familiarity was comforting, as was the sound of hooves clip-clopping on concrete and the continuous chatter in the yard. Tilly knew Silver Shoe was where she belonged, horse or no horse.

'Hey! There you are!' called Angela.

She was lugging a bag of feed from the barn to the feed room. She put it down, came straight over to Tilly and gave her a hug.

'My best worker! I'm glad you're here. It's getting busy.'

'What shall I do?' said Tilly.

It felt weird to ask such a question. Normally, Tilly had a routine, tending to Magic's needs: mucking out, feeding, grooming, tacking up, exercising, training, checking for injuries, the list went on.

Now she had none of that. She felt a bit bewildered.

'Well, for starters, Autumn Glory needs to stretch his legs while Mia's on holiday,' said Angela. 'Perhaps you could trot him around the outdoor arena, maybe give him a jump. And when you're done, you could turn out Solo and Thumbelina.'

'Okay,' said Tilly.

'Then after that, I'll meet you in the clubhouse for a hot chocolate.'

Tilly wandered over to the tack room to collect Autumn Glory's saddle and bridle.

Autumn belonged to her good friend, Mia, who she'd known since she'd first started coming to Silver Shoe. In fact, she'd helped Mia choose Autumn. Mia had been looking for a new horse for ages, but hadn't found one that suited her, then they'd found Autumn, just as they'd been about to give up hope.

She carried the saddle to his stable, then led him out.

'Hello, Autumn,' she said, stroking his chestnut coat. 'Are you missing Mia?'

Autumn twitched.

'I know how you feel.'

Tilly sighed and positioned Autumn's bridle over his nose, then hoisted the saddle over his back. She'd ridden him before lots of times. He had a lovely temperament. He was easy-going, willing to try things and always cooperative. He was an ideal horse in many ways.

But he wasn't Magic.

Tilly pulled on her riding helmet and attached the strap. She mounted and nudged Autumn forward. It felt good to be back in the saddle. It felt natural. Unfortunately, however, it made her miss Magic more than ever. She knew Magic so well, every bone, every muscle. As she rode towards the arena, she longed for the feel of his exuberant trot, his rhythm, the slope of his neck, the width of his back. Compared to Magic, Autumn felt alien.

By the time Tilly got to the clubhouse, Angela already had two mugs of frothy chocolate waiting.

'How did you get on?' she asked.

'Fine,' said Tilly, mustering as much enthusiasm as she could, which wasn't much at all.

Tilly sat on the old sofa and caught a glimpse of a programme for Weston Park lying on the coffee table – another painful reminder of everything that she'd lost. She quickly covered the programme with a magazine and avoided all thoughts of Kya excitedly getting ready for the event.

'You know, we'll do what we can to get you and Magic back together,' Angela said, well aware of Tilly's mood. 'I can't see someone like Fred Webb having the patience for Magic's antics. I'm doing what I can, believe me.'

'Thanks, Angela,' Tilly replied, but she couldn't imagine how Angela was going to be able to stop Fred Webb selling Magic to a dealer from Crewe. Maybe he'd already done it. That was too much for Tilly to bear.

'I know from experience,' Angela went on. 'I know how painful it can be. Horses will come and go. Some of them will barely have an impact on you, but some will break your heart and make you feel as if you've lost the only thing that's ever mattered. But you will always be a rider. Remember that, won't you?'

Tilly nodded and managed a half-hearted smile.

'By the way, you'll be back tomorrow, won't you?'

'Er, I think so.'

'Make sure,' said Angela. 'Make sure.'

Nine

That night, Tilly dreamed she was riding Magic to triumph at Weston Park. It was so vivid. She could hear the crowd, feel the breeze and smell the grass on the cross-country course. She woke up suddenly, realising it wasn't real. She lay awake in the moonlight, twiddling her horsehair bracelets and wondering what her beautiful horse was up to. She thought about what Angela had said, about always being a rider and having to get used to different horses and used to change. She understood what Angela meant, but at the same time, she couldn't imagine life without Magic.

She picked up the photo of them jumping a triple bar. They were perfect together. They were meant to be. No other horse would be the same.

'I'll never forget you,' she whispered, caressing the photo.

Then she caught sight of the date on her clock. Two days to go until the first dressage tests at Weston Park.

'It should be you and me,' she said, gazing at Magic's photo. 'It should have been us.'

When morning came, a weight of sorrow still lingered. Tilly was even less energetic about getting ready than the day before.

'Silver Shoe today?' said her mum, at breakfast.

'Don't know if I feel like it,' said Tilly.

'But you'll feel good when you're there –'

'Will I?'

Tilly's mum looked worried.

'What can we do with you?' she said, plying Tilly with fresh juice and scrambled eggs. 'It's as if your life-force is being drained!'

'That's how it feels, Mum,' said Tilly, pushing the scrambled egg around the plate. 'Magic is my life-force. Without him, I feel empty.'

Her mum squeezed her shoulder.

'Take it one day at a time,' she said. 'Things will start to feel easier eventually.'

Tilly gave an unconvinced sigh and distracted herself with her phone. Unfortunately, the first thing she came across was an update from Kya – a picture of her and Bastion looking polished and groomed and smiley, with the caption:

All ready for Weston Park. Good luck to everyone competing. It's going to be an amazing week. Feeling blessed (unlike some). xxxxxx

Tilly stiffened with anger.

She thought about throwing her phone across the room, then she thought about throwing Kya across the room, then decided it wasn't worth her emotions. She didn't need to get sucked into Kya's shallow spite. She just needed to grit her teeth, hold her head up high, and keep going forward.

'Mum,' she said, 'actually, could I have a lift to Silver Shoe, please?'

'Of course,' said her mum.

Despite Angela's keenness for Tilly to spend the day in the yard, when Tilly arrived she was nowhere to be seen. In fact, the yard was quiet, so Tilly decided to get on with whatever needed doing. She checked the board in the tack room to see which horses still needed mucking out, then set to work.

Half an hour later, she caught a glimpse of Angela marching out of the clubhouse. It looked as if she had something on her mind. She headed straight for the front gate, where a shiny silver 4x4 had just pulled up – the one that had visited before. Tilly stopped sweeping up outside the stable she had just mucked out and watched.

The couple, the brown-haired lady and the grey-bearded man, climbed out and greeted Angela. A moment later, a familiar old horsebox, pulled up behind. Tilly was puzzled for a moment, then overwhelmed by

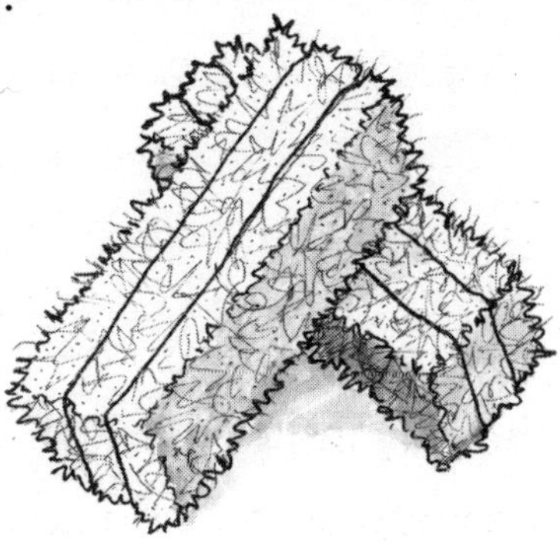

a strange, lightheaded feeling – she knew that horsebox. It was Fred Webb's. What was going on? *Something* was going on!

The next few moments happened in a blur. Fred Webb got out and shook hands with Angela and the couple. He was dressed in a sort-of smart suit and was being far more polite than usual. The couple were smiling. Angela was smiling. The couple handed Fred Webb a large envelope. Then there was a whinny from the horsebox.

Magic!

Tilly dropped her broom and raced forwards.

'Magic! Is it Magic? Is he in there?'

Angela spun round and grinned.

'Hi, Tilly. Yes, Magic's in there.'

Tilly smiled nervously.

'I – I don't understand. What's going on?'

'Tilly, this is Mr and Mrs Armon-Jones.'

The couple smiled.

'They've been great supporters of Silver

Shoe for years. I told them about you and Magic a little while ago –'

'We own a lot of horses,' Mrs Armon-Jones explained. 'Recently, we've decided we want to invest in young talent, in the riders and horses of the future.'

Tilly's heart started to beat fast.

'Does this mean –?'

'We came to Silver Shoe a few weeks ago,' said Mr Armon-Jones, 'to talk to Angela about investment opportunities.'

He nodded at Angela. Angela smiled.

'She was quick to point you out to us – and your fantastic grey, Magic Spirit,' said Mrs Armon-Jones, taking up the story. 'We could see the potential immediately. We were very excited, but we weren't quite ready to make a decision. And then, early this week when Angela phoned to tell us that Magic was about to be sold, we realised we had to act fast. So here we are.'

'You mean you're buying Magic?' said Tilly, eyes glassy with tears. 'You're buying Magic, so that I can ride him . . . *forever*?'

The couple nodded. Fred Webb clutched his envelope of money. Tilly blinked.

'I – I don't know what to say,' she said.

On impulse, she flung her arms around the couple and squeezed them into a hug. Over their shoulders, she caught Angela's eye. Angela just winked.

'Thank you,' Tilly mouthed. 'Thank you!'

Fred Webb coughed.

'No offence,' he said, attempting politeness. 'But I've got to get to the bank. So, if you could take the nag, then we're square, yes?'

'No problem,' said Tilly, dashing round to the back of the horsebox. 'And by the way, that "nag" has a name.'

But Fred Webb was too busy

peering into his envelope, counting his takings.

Tilly undid the bolt as quickly as she could. She flung the ramp down. Magic was in the back, staring at the light. The moment he saw Tilly he pulled at his ropes. He nearly broke them trying to get to her. She threw her arms around his neck.

Tears poured down her cheeks, but finally they weren't tears of sorrow. They were tears of joy.

As Tilly led Magic down the ramp into the yard, Angela and the Armon-Joneses gave them a round of applause. It was a relief to see Fred Webb's dirty horsebox drive away.

'He didn't seem like a particularly animal loving person,' said Mr Armon-Jones.

'He wasn't,' said Angela. 'But that's all in the past now. This is the future.'

'Absolutely,' said Mr Armon-Jones. 'I predict great things.'

He reached and stroked Magic's nose.

Magic responded by whickering contentedly. *A good sign,* thought Tilly, knowing it wasn't usual for Magic to be affectionate to strangers.

'He likes you,' she said.

'Because I like him,' said Mr Armon-Jones. 'I've been crazy about horses since I was a boy. I'm looking forward to getting to know you, Tilly. We both are. We knew from the moment we saw you working in the arena with your friends that you had a spark about you.'

'Thanks,' said Tilly.

'We've agreed that it's best all round if Magic stays here at Silver Shoe Farm,' said Mrs Armon-Jones. 'That way you and he can train all you need. But we also have a fantastic stable yard of our own, about an hour away. Feel free to visit whenever you like.'

'It's amazing,' said Angela. 'It's like a luxury hotel for horses.'

Tilly grinned. She couldn't believe it.

'All we ask is that you give us regular updates on your progress. Leave the money to us. You focus on your riding. And if there's any other help you need, planning your competition schedule, overseas travel expenses, finding sponsorship, that sort of thing, let us know. We've made a lot of money through horses over the years, but now we want to use it to make a difference to talented young riders like you.'

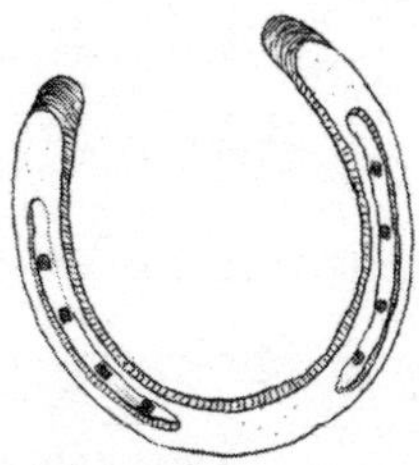

'Thank you,' said Tilly, eyes sparkling. 'Thank you so much. You don't know how much this means to me and Magic.'

She gazed at Magic. He gazed back at her. Everything felt right again.

'So what's next?' said Mrs Armon-Jones. 'Obviously the eventing season is coming to an end –'

'Not quite,' said Angela.

Tilly looked up.

'What were the criteria for you competing in Weston Park? That the dispute about Magic's ownership is cleared up? I think we can safely say that's sorted now.'

'But –?'

'Starts in two days.'

'They've given my place away,' said Tilly.

'I think they'll happily give it back, if it means they can have their star rider on the team.'

'We haven't trained. We haven't practised for over a week.'

Angela scoffed.

'Come on, Tilly. You know that's not going to be an issue. You and Magic have clocked up enough training, enough experience and enough of a bond to be able to pull it out of the hat.'

'It would be lovely to come and see you both compete together,' said Mr

Armon-Jones encouragingly.

Magic pawed the ground with his hoof and snorted.

'Let's do it then,' said Tilly, electrified by the thought.

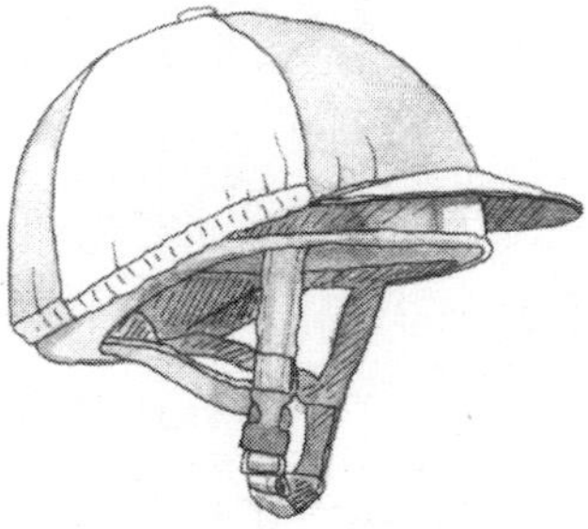

Ten

Weston Park, a beautiful country estate, was one of the grandest Tilly had ever been to. She'd seen pictures of the house and gardens on websites, but up close they were more impressive than she'd imagined.

'I feel like a pro,' she giggled to Brook, as they dropped the ramp of the horsebox.

'And you'll ride like a pro!' he said.

'Thanks.' She paused. 'You know I really appreciate you coming with me.'

'Wouldn't miss it for the world,' said Brook. 'After everything you and I have been through, we deserve to enjoy it. And you and Magic deserve to have a great competition.'

They gave each other a hug then led Magic to his temporary stable. As soon as Magic sensed the atmosphere and saw the clusters of horses being led around the event site, he grew skittish.

'He's excited,' said Tilly, giving him a pat. 'He's raring to go.'

'And I expect he's pretty relieved to be back with you. What better way to celebrate than by winning Weston Park?'

'Winning?'

Brook smiled.

'Yes, winning.'

Brook had offered to stay with Tilly and Magic for all three days of the competition, so he could help with grooming, sponging and last-minute advice. Tilly was thrilled to have him there.

She hadn't seen Kya since that day she'd swept out of the sand school and was dreading their next encounter. With Brook by her side, she felt she could be more confident.

'Okay,' said Brook, as he gave her a leg up onto Magic. 'This is it. Last-minute checks.'

He gave Magic's coat a quick rub to make sure it gleamed, wiped around his mouth, flicked a speck of mud off his front leg, then buffed the tips of Tilly's riding boots with a cloth.

'Straighten your riding helmet. There's nothing worse than a wonky hat.'

Tilly adjusted her hat and smoothed her plaited bun.

'You both look perfect,' said Brook. 'Now, show the judges what you're capable of.'

As Tilly trotted around the outside of the dressage arena awaiting the bell to signal her start, she was delighted to see a crowd of supporters waiting to cheer her on. Her mum and dad and brother were there, along with Brook's parents. Harry, Ben and Anna were standing beside them, eating hot dogs.

'Go Tilly!' chanted Ben and Anna, while Harry gave her the hugest smile.

Her stomach filled with butterflies, but it was hard to tell whether they were caused by Harry's presence, or by pre-competition nerves.

'Next into the arena we have Tiger Lily Redbrow riding Mr and Mrs Armon-Jones' Magic Spirit,' the commentator announced, as the bell rang.

They trotted up the centre line to a straight, square halt, immediately impressing the judges. Tilly realised she had no need to worry about her and Magic missing training time together. Despite their separation, they were perfectly in tune with one another.

They seemed to dance their way through the dressage test. Their free walk on a long rein was the most relaxed it had ever been. Their serpentines were rhythmic, and their counter canter was balanced and straight. When the test was complete, Tilly had to bite her lip to stop from whooping with joy. Instead, she gave a polite salute to all three judges.

She dismounted in the collecting area, where Brook was waiting with a wet sponge.

'You were both awesome,' he said.

Magic whickered.

'Don't look now, but Kya and Bastion are in the arena.'

'How are they looking?' asked Tilly.

Brook peered over her shoulder.

'Pretty slick, I'm afraid. Although I don't think Bastion looks that happy. He and Kya don't have the relationship you and Magic have.'

They spent the night at a nearby hotel. Tilly was delighted when she realised Anna, Ben, and Harry and their families were all booked in at the same place. They decided to have dinner together in the hotel's restaurant.

'This is so much fun,' whispered Anna, as she glanced through her menu. 'Shame Kya's missing out.'

'Where's she staying?' asked Brook.

'Some place that belongs to her parents' friends,' replied Harry.

'Hey, check this out,' said Ben, interrupting. He thrust his phone in front of Tilly. 'The competitive rivalry between you and Kya has become a news story.'

Tilly looked. He'd pulled up a press release from a popular eventing website. It was about Tilly and Magic the Rescue Horse going head to head with Kelston Equestrian ambassador Kya Mackensie and Bastion.

Tilly cringed.

'Where did they get all this information about us?'

'Don't knock it,' said Anna. 'A bit of media attention will help get your name out there.'

'The important question is,' said Harry, with a wink, 'who's going to win?'

Next morning, the sky was bright blue with not a cloud in sight – ideal conditions for cross-country. Brook gave Magic his breakfast and got everything organised while Tilly, similar to Livvy in Luhmühlen, walked the cross-country course for a third time, this time on her own so she was one hundred per cent sure of all her lines. She knew she couldn't afford to make a single mistake and, with Kya on her tail, she definitely didn't want any time penalties.

Luckily, the course suited Magic perfectly. The jumps were well spaced and there were plenty of stretches where he could notch up speed. There was, however, a rather nasty-looking trakehner right at the end. Tilly breathed deeply and told herself not to fret – although she felt a little worried about trakehners, she and Magic had conquered them. She just needed to remember what she'd learned.

Tilly gave herself plenty of time to get organised. She always felt that when she was nervous, she needed everything in place: helmet, hairnet, back protector, stop watch. She didn't want any last minute stress.

Having got ready she found a quiet corner away from everyone so she could run through the course one last time in her head, imagining how to ride each fence at the correct speed on the right line.

Just as she was finishing, she heard someone mention her name. A couple of journalists and a photographer came over. They'd spotted her leaning against a tree.

'Hello, Tilly,' said one of them. 'How's your preparation going?'

'Er, fine, thanks,' said Tilly, stunned.

'What do you think of your chances?' said another.

The photographer started snapping pictures.

'Tell us how you feel about Kya Mackensie. Do you think she's got what it takes?'

'And is it good to have Magic Spirit back? You and he have been on quite a journey together, haven't you? It's a great story, by the way.'

'Are you enjoying being one of the hot favourites in the Junior Championships?'

The barrage of questions was too much. Tilly stood up and backed away.

'I – I'm sorry,' she said. 'Can't talk now. I've got to compete.'

Then she ran as fast as she could back to Magic and Brook.

'You won't believe this,' she said, throwing her arms around Magic's shoulders. 'I've just been hounded by interviewers. I guess Kya and I really are the talk of the competition.'

'Don't let it distract you though,' said Brook. 'Keep your focus.'

'I will,' said Tilly.

She mounted then walked Magic to the start. She did her best to think of the ride ahead of her, but all around her she could hear her name being called. Lots of people – friends, family and people she didn't even know – were cheering her on. It felt weird and amazing.

'Come on, boy,' she said, gripping Magic's reins. 'Let's give them a reason to cheer!'

They cruised around the course faster than

usual, going up a gear. She knew time was tight and that in order to ride the fences at the speed they were used to, she had to go faster in between and shave off corners. The jumps came up quickly but she and Magic tackled each out of a lovely forward rhythm, making everything look effortless and smooth.

'Just a normal log,' Tilly whispered to herself as they approached the trakehner. 'Forget about the ditch underneath. Take it straight.'

Magic sailed over it and landed safely. This time, Tilly did whoop with joy.

'I love you, Magic!' she cried. 'You're the best horse ever!'

At the end of cross-country day, thanks to an amazing fast, faultless round, she and Magic were at the top of the leader board. They were thrilled – but slightly troubled that Kya and Bastion were only two penalty points behind, which was less than a show jump fault.

'We have to hold on to our lead,' she whispered as she checked Magic one last time before going to bed. 'So much counts on us winning. If we pull it off, we'll do Brook proud. We'll impress Mr and Mrs Armon-Jones. And we'll show Kya and the rest of the country exactly what a so-called "stolen" rescue horse can do.'

Magic shook his head and let out a whinny.

'That's right, boy!' said Tilly.

Unfortunately, a horse that had lost a shoe on the cross-country failed the final vet's inspection due to being a little sore, otherwise all were passed fit and well the following morning. Magic towed Tilly along the trot up strip as if he hadn't done anything the day before. Angela had been correct in saying a fit horse doesn't lose fitness in a week.

As the crowds gathered for the show jumping that afternoon, there was more talk about the showdown between Tilly and Kya. Everywhere Tilly went, she could see people looking at her and whispering. She tried not to pay attention. She didn't want any added pressure. She simply wanted to focus on the jumps.

Kya, however, seemed pleased with all the attention. While Tilly was busy walking the show jumping course, she spotted her at the edge of the arena, dressed in a Kelston Equestrian jacket and breeches, chatting and smiling as her photo was taken. She noticed Tilly watching her, gave her a quick icy glare, then suddenly started smiling even more, batting her eyelids and flicking her hair.

'She's playing up to the cameras,' whispered Brook. 'What she obviously hasn't realised is that the course is about to be closed for walking. The first horse is due to jump in a couple of minutes.'

As soon as Kya realised she'd missed the walk, her smile became a look of panic. *Not a great way to prepare for such an important show jumping round,* Tilly couldn't help thinking.

After an erratic, flustered warm-up, Kya and Bastion struggled into the first few jumps. Tilly had done her final warm-up fence. She was last to go, so next into the ring. She and Brook looked on.

'They have not got a good rhythm,' said Brook. 'They may have the gear and look the part, but they don't have the connection and partnership that you and Magic share.'

Bastion made it over most of the jumps, but

it was clear he was jumping because he was so genuine, not because he wanted to. And in the final combination, their effort unravelled completely when Kya took a long stride to the first element. Bastion tried his hardest, chipped in a tiny stride, but was unable to get his legs out of the way so they had two poles down.

'Ouch!' said Tilly.

'Ew!' said Brook, then he broke into a grin. 'You have more leeway now – the title is there for you.'

'Unless I have a disaster,' said Tilly, trying to stay focused.

'You won't have a disaster,' said Brook confidently.

Tilly looked up at Magic. She knew Brook was right.

As they were about to enter the show jumping arena, Mr and Mrs Armon-Jones caught up with them. Their eyes were twinkling with pride.

'Good luck, Tilly!' said Mr Armon-Jones.

'You're doing brilliantly!' said Mrs Armon-Jones.

'And what a horse!' added Mr Armon-Jones, giving Magic a pat.

'Thanks,' said Tilly. 'It's because of you that we're here . . .'

'Oh no,' said Mrs Armon-Jones. 'Really, Tilly, it's because of *you*.'

With the Armon-Joneses' support in her mind, Tilly cantered into the arena. The audience fell silent.

'This is it,' she whispered to Magic, as she saluted to the judges. 'Our chance to shine!'

She knew they didn't need to deliver a flawless round – Kya had given herself a bundle of penalties – but they did it anyway. Fence after fence, they jumped clear. They didn't just jump, they practically flew.

As Magic cleared the final oxer, the crowd

roared. It was the biggest cheer Tilly had ever heard. She punched the air joyfully, then rode round to the side of the arena where her family and friends were waiting.

'You did it!' said Harry, blowing her a kiss.

'You are both stars,' said Brook, with a tear in his eye.

'That's my girl, Under 18 National Champion!' said her dad.

But Tilly, lost in the moment, just smiled and stroked Magic's shoulder.

'Well done, boy,' she whispered.

'Long live Team Magic!'

World Horse Welfare

World Horse Welfare is an international charity which works to improve the horse-human partnership in all of its forms: helping horses in need, horses in sport and leisure, and horses used in work and production both in the UK and worldwide.

For almost a century, we have improved welfare through hands-on care, research, education and influence and by working with owners, communities, organisations and governments, improving welfare standards and stamping out suffering.

World Horse Welfare runs the country's largest equine rescue and rehoming scheme; taking in over 300 horses and ponies each year to its four UK centres, aiming to find each one a loving new home after they have been expertly rehabilitated.

By supporting World Horse Welfare you are helping horses who need it most.

Find out more: www.worldhorsewelfare.org

Pippa's Eventing Life

1968 7 October, my birthday
My first pony was Pepsi 11.2hh, followed by Flighty 12.2hh, then Jeremy Fisher 13.1hh

1982 At 14 years old, my first horse was Sir Barnaby 16.1hh

1984 At 16, I started affiliated eventing

1985 I was working and training with Ruth McMullen in Norfolk

1986 I represented Great Britain in the Junior European Championships and won my team medal with Airborne

1987 European Young Rider Champion with Sir Barnaby

1988 Young Rider European Championships, team gold with Sir Barnaby

1989 Young Rider European Championship, team gold and individual silver with Sir Barnaby

1990 A string of 10 horses to work with. Many of their owners have supported me throughout my career

1993 Married show jumper, William Funnell, and moved to Cobbett's Farm

1997 I was selected for the senior team with my little coloured horse, Bits and Pieces

1999 European Championships, team and individual gold with Supreme Rock

2000 Olympic Games Sydney, NSW, team silver with Supreme Rock

2001 European Championships, team and individual gold with Supreme Rock

2002 1st at Badminton with Supreme Rock
World Championships, team bronze with Supreme Rock

2003 1st at Kentucky with Primmore's Pride
1st at Badminton for the second time with Supreme Rock
1st at Burghley with Primmore's Pride
First winner of Rolex Grand Slam – three consecutive wins at Badminton, Burghley, Kentucky
European Championships, team gold and individual bronze with Walk On Star
No: 1 ranked rider in the world
Sunday Times Sports Woman of the Year

2004 Athens Olympics, team silver and individual bronze with Primmore's Pride

2005 1st at Badminton, my third win there. This time with Primmore's Pride
European Championships with Ensign
Awarded an MBE in the Birthday Honours list

2008 Eventing World Cup Final, 2nd place with Ensign

2010 World Equestrian Games, 5th individual with Redesigned

2013 European Championships with Mirage D'Elle

2015 European Championships, team silver with Sandman 7

2016 Rio de Janeiro Olympics with Billy the Biz

2019 1st at Burghley with MGH Grafton Street
European Championships, team silver with Majas Hope
BT Action Sports Woman of the Year

2021 Bicton CCI 5*, 2nd and 5th places with Billy Walk On and Majas Hope

2023 1st at Bramham CCI 4* with MCS Maverick

2024 9th at Badminton with MCS Maverick

PIPPA'S PONY TALES

Tilly lives, breathes and dreams horses. The only thing missing from life with her adoptive family is a pony of her own.

When Red Admiral, a young, injured racehorse, arrives at Silver Shoe Farm, it's not long before Tilly helps him on the road to recovery.

Tilly is thrilled to start riding lessons at Silver Shoe Farm.

Everyone at Silver Shoe Farm is excited for the London International Horse Show. Can Tilly help calm a fiery stallion who no one seems able to get near?

The team at Silver Shoe Farm are proud to work with the World Horse Welfare charity to care for neglected horses.

Tilly is getting ready for her first Pony Club competition. She's excited and nervous and so is Brook who is competing on Solo.

On a visit to Angela's favourite horse, Pride and Joy, Tilly is fascinated to discover what it's like to have a special partnership with an eventing superstar!

On holiday, it takes all Tilly's skills, and a brave and gentle horse called Neptune to make a daring sea rescue.

When the dainty and elegant show pony Parkview Pickle arrives at Silver Shoe Farm, Tilly knows straight away that something is wrong.

PIPPA'S PONY TALES

When a mischievous circus pony comes to stay at Silver Shoe Farm, Tilly soon realises they have no idea what they have let themselves in for.

A sleepover at the stables reveals just how far some people are prepared to go to get close to a Derby winner.

Finding the perfect horse is difficult and Tilly wonders if her friend Mia's dream will ever come true.

At World Horse Welfare, Tilly meets neglected shire horse Goliath, and she's determined to help him find a new home.

Naughty pony Buttons is coming to Silver Shoe Farm because his owner just doesn't know what to do with him. They need Tilly's help – and fast!

When gentle pony, Rusty, arrives at Silver Shoe Farm, Tilly senses something special about him.

There's a VIP guest at Silver Shoe Farm – retired police horse, Royal Flame.

Tilly wins a horse safari trip to Africa, and helps rescue abandoned zebra foal, Stripy.

Tilly can't believe she's going to the Kentucky Horse Trials to see her brother Brook compete.

Points of a horse

A horse's height is measured in **hands** from the ground up to its withers. A hand is 4 inches/10.6 centimetres.

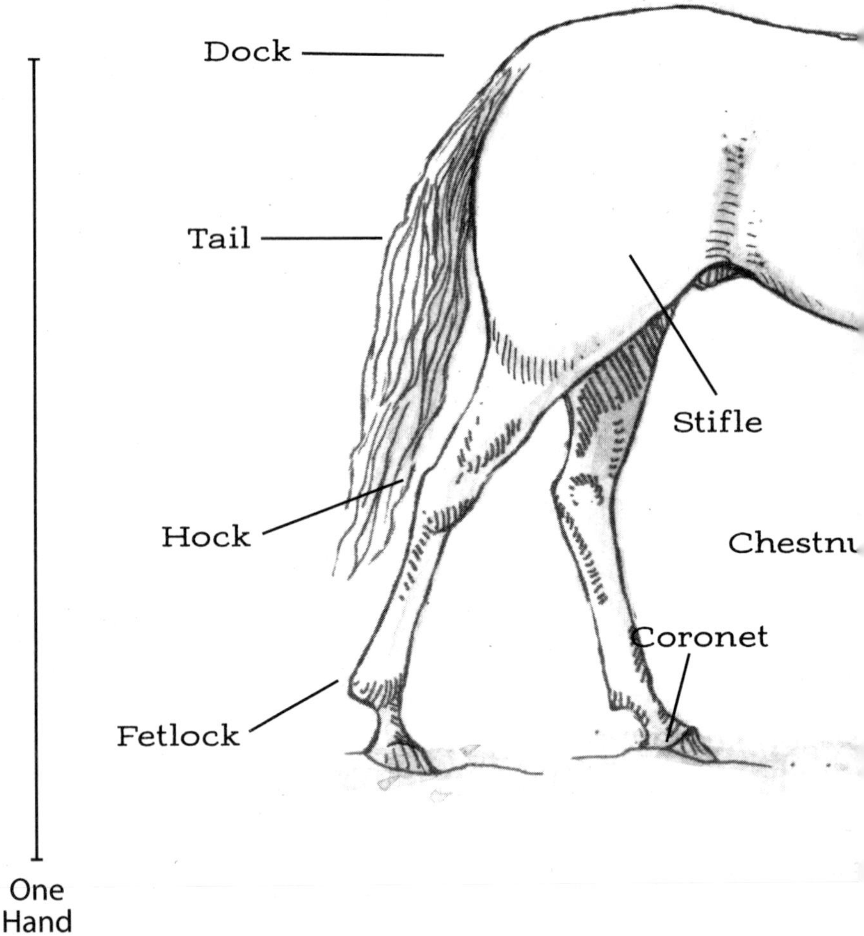

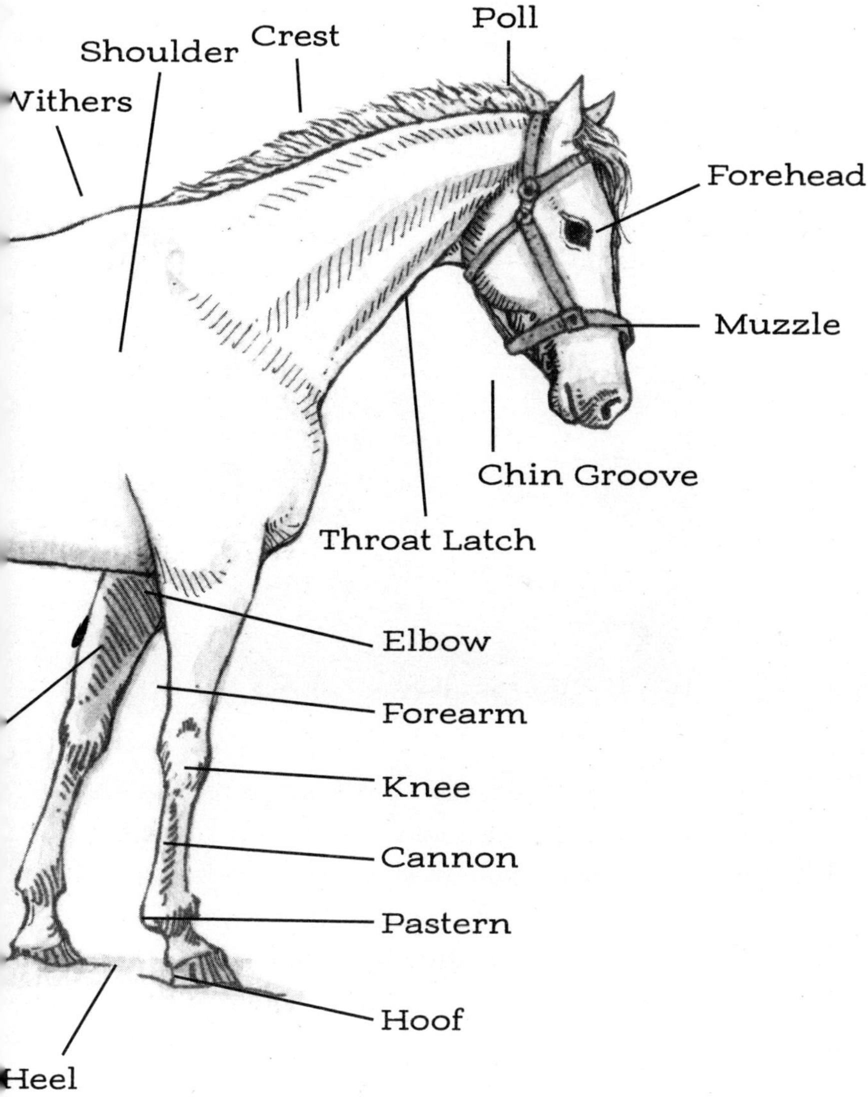
Poll
Shoulder
Crest
Withers
Forehead
Muzzle
Chin Groove
Throat Latch
Elbow
Forearm
Knee
Cannon
Pastern
Hoof
Heel

PIPPA'S PONY TALES

Tilly and Magic Spirit have been chosen to take part in the Pony Club Eventing Championships. She and her new teammates, and their horses, are put through their paces in dressage, cross-country and show jumping, as they discover how to work together.

Tilly, Magic Spirit and the rest of the Junior Squad are training with a top eventer for a week. There's a lot of hard work and a lot to learn if they are all to achieve their dreams. To be the best, you have to train like the best, and Tilly and her friends' team spirit is pushed to the limit.

PIPPA'S PONY TALES

Tilly has an exciting opportunity to groom for a top eventer at an international event. It's inspiring to be around so many famous horses and riders, although she misses her horse Magic Spirit and the Silver Shoe stables. Then disaster strikes, and she realises how much she needs teamwork to turn the day around.

Tilly is excited to be picked for the Novice Championships, but her dreams turn to nightmares when someone who claims to be Magic Spirit's real owner unexpectedly appears on the scene. He demands the return of his horse. Tilly is heartbroken. Will she and Magic Spirit ever be reunited?